words by
SUSAN VERDE

pictures by
KATiE KATH

My Kicks

A SNEAKER STORY!

Abrams Books for Young Readers
New York

Mom looked down at my feet and shook her head.

"Those shoes have seen their day!"

"They are old,
falling apart, stinky,
and sticky . . .

. . . torn in places,
with shredded laces.

It's time for a **NEW** pair."

"But, Mom, there's **NOTHING** like an **OLD** pair of kicks! I won't give them up. No way! No how!"

They may be worn and torn, but they've got stories to tell.

I'll never forget how I learned to tie my laces
on these old sneaks!

First just knots . . .

. . . then bows and doubles.

Maybe the ends *are* frayed—but how would
you look after being all tied and twisted?

I'll never forget that summer storm. That's how I got those wet spots. I was faster than lightning as I ran home, hitting every puddle in my path.

Splashes as big as ocean waves!

I'll never forget my first time on my skateboard! Building up speed and finding my balance! That's how I got that tear right there.

It was awesome! I **RULED** that day!

I'll never forget the
time I was an artist,
paintbrush in hand.

Drops fell onto the canvas, and then onto
my sneaks! That's how they got all those
colorful splatters.

A work of **ART!**

I'll never forget the taste of that Popsicle last summer. Sitting on my stoop, trying to catch the drips swirling down my arm.

That's how I got that stain over my big toe. **SPLAT!**

Deee-licious!

I'll never forget those days playing outside and trying to climb the biggest tree. Whatever the game, those sneaks were right there with me.

I'll never forget the dog that left a "present" on the sidewalk.

OOPS!

That was a stinky one!

These sneakers have soul in their soles.
Joy in each hole. A certain stick-to-the-
sidewalk from gooey gum.

They might be soggy and funky, the tongue flapping,
the laces dragging, but they are irreplaceable,
a perfect fit, molded to my feet! I **CAN'T** let them go.

Mom said,
"How about these?"

NAH.

Mom said,
"What about those?"

NO WAY.

Mom said, "We aren't leaving without a new pair."

HMM . . .

Maybe if I try them on,
she'll see that nothing
compares!

I slip on the right . . .

Well . . .
ALL RIGHT.

I slip on the left . . .

Maybe these don't
feel so bad.

Maybe I'll just try a
little jump right here.
WHOA—pretty high!

Maybe I'll just take a lap
around the store.
WHOOSH—that was fast!

Maybe I'll take a longer look.

Shiny, shimmery,
laces long and strong.
I could do some serious tying.
Double, maybe triple, bows.

Maybe . . .

With these shoes, I can push that skateboard with power. I'll ride all day long.

With these shoes, I can run faster in a storm. Not a drop of rain will touch me.

With these shoes, I can sidestep those paint drops and Popsicle drips.

Or maybe they'll be the perfect canvas.

With these shoes,
I can dribble the soccer
ball around the field.

Everyone will notice
my fancy footwork.

With these shoes, no one will catch me in tag.
I'll never be "it" on the playground.

With these shoes, I'll be the champion tree climber.

Is there a cat or a ball stuck up there? I'll be a hero!

With these shoes, I can be the longest
long jumper on the sidewalk.

I'll leap right over
those doggy presents.

Mom says, "Well . . . what do you think?"

"There's **NOTHING** like a **NEW** pair of kicks!"

To my own fellas, who
know how to wear the heck
out of their favorite kicks
—S. V.

To my husband, father, and
father-in-law, who are loath
to part with their old kicks
—K. K.

The art in this book was created using ink and watercolor.

Cataloging-in-Publication Data has been applied for
and may be obtained from the Library of Congress.
ISBN: 978-1-4197-2309-4

Printed and bound in China
10 9 8 7 6 5 4 3 2 1

Abrams Books for Young Readers are available at special discounts when
purchased in quantity for premiums and promotions as well as fundraising
or educational use. Special editions can also be created to specification. For
details, contact specialsales@abramsbooks.com or the address below.

ABRAMS The Art of Books
115 West 18th Street, New York, NY 10011
abramsbooks.com

JUN   2017